THE
CIVIL WAR

With a Twist

James Flanagan

DEDICATION

*This book is dedicated to all who are fans of
"The Twilight Zone."*

Table Of Contents

About the Author

Jim is a professional storyteller. He has told in Ohio, Pennsylvania, Virginia, Washington DC, and Ireland. He teaches writing at The Thurber House and has been the storyteller at Nationwide Children's Hospital in Columbus, Oh.

He has written 4 books geared toward grades 4-10. He is a retired middle school principal and coach.

I HAVE ALWAYS WANTED
TO SEE A GHOST

Darkness was coming. I was on a strange undertaking, assuming it would go well. But I had butterflies in my stomach. I spent the last ten years attending lectures, going on haunted tours, and spending time at libraries. I was looking for an excellent spot to see a ghost. Finally, I was onto something. I have excellent information based on eyewitness accounts and research, but they could be rumors too.

My family thinks I am going overboard. I have explained that as a police detective, it helps hone my skills. They did not buy it. I stopped talking about my hobby in the office. If I talked about my hobby, they smiled and went back to work. To my office, I was bordering on becoming a whacko.

I believed this trip would *finally* show them.

I headed to Sharpsburg, following Maryland Route 34. I waited until there is no traffic and turned onto a road bordering the National Park. I parked my car on a blocked-off road, hiding it well from the view. The Antietam National Battlefield, the object of my investigation, was in front of me—across the road.

I took a deep breath, left my car, and walked to the park's fence line. Earlier, I found a bent-down span of the fence. I climbed over a low part and moved to a tree line. I sat down and waited a while to ensure I wasn't observed by the park rangers with their night vision glasses. I picked this spot because pine trees screen me. The field I was going to is not far from the fence line. I visited the National Park three times in the last week. I looked for and found the right spot.

After a few minutes, I got up and moved out of the cover toward an acre of field boxed in by forest and fence. The area is approximately 5 acres. The field is free of the shadows of the trees. It had the look of a golf course, the grass green and lush. It was different from the photograph Matthew Brady took here in 1862. Then, the field was strewn with bodies. The fence was torn down, and craters were at the edge of the area.

I had heard of several undisturbed Civil War graves in many places on the field. After the battle of Antietam, Most of the bodies, according to my research, were Confederate. They were buried in groups, covered over, and forgotten. The field remained relatively untouched for years afterward, and the men remained nameless. Of course, the park officials know the graves are there, but their exact positions are unknown. The National Park Service has decided to leave the sites in peace.

I found cover on the edge of the field. It was beautiful, green, and mowed. I sat down and waited in the trees. It was a good night for ghosts. Clouds partially hid the moon. There was a ground fog forming at the far end of the field. It was eerily quiet. It reminded me of an old black-and-white TV ghost movie. My nerves were on the verge of jumping.

After being in that spot for a few minutes, I heard the summer sounds start up again, the crickets, the birds in the trees, and an occasional owl hoot. It was comforting. The field was accepting me. I watched for any indication that "ghosts were about." Sitting, I thought of the usually polite, smartly dressed, and helpful park rangers. But they would take a very harsh view of anyone being on the grounds after hours, snooping around, or "disturbing the dead."

If they could see me now, they would be less than kind. There would be heavy fines and confiscation of any equipment and maybe jail if I were caught. I laughed, thinking I was more afraid of the park rangers than the ghosts in some ways.

I had gone over the entire expedition in my mind. It is the part of the field I was sure was haunted. I used Matthew Brady's famous picture of the dead and read his vivid, gruesome description. This field was in the same place as in the picture. The bodies of the Confederate dead were lined up, sprawled out, and waiting for burial.

It is THE field, and tonight is THE night. It is September, fall, and chilly.

I had thought about what I would do and say if a ghost happened to be nearby. But even as I was ready to go onto the field, I still had doubts. "What would the ghost look like? "What would it say?" Would I run or stand in shock?"

Well, it was ShowTime, so I stepped out into the field. I stood and scanned the far fence and then the area. I waited. I scanned again. I waited. Thirty minutes passed. I decided it was not haunted, just another field on a late summer evening. There was nothing here.

Out of the night, I heard a vehicle at the other end of the field. I dashed back into the tree line and hid behind a tree. A four-wheel, all-terrain car drove out of the trees and crossed to the middle of the field. Two park rangers got out and looked all around. They seemed pleased that there was no one about and drove off. They had not seen me. I could get away.

It was time to leave. I quickly backtracked to the place I had entered the park. When I reached that spot, someone was already there. The person seemed to be waiting. I hid for a minute but realized I should stand up and go to the fence. I was caught, the rangers had somehow seen me, and I might as well face it.

The person appeared in a haze, wavy, similar to the heat radiating off the highway. As I moved up, he became clearer, distinct. The ranger looked at me and spoke, but I could not understand his words. The person spoke with a strong accent, perhaps southern. This could be a re-enactor of staying character.

I continued to walk toward the person very cautiously.

But I soon realized he was not dressed in a ranger uniform. He had no hat, bag, or flashlight. I stepped closer to get a better look. This person in front of the fence was dressed in a Confederate uniform. I noticed his clothes were in bad shape. The Confederate's right arm hung heavily by his side. The man was young. His face was smudged with black powder. He looked like a player out of a movie. He stared at me with blank eyes. He was filthy and unkempt. The rebel soldier looked at the ground, then the fence, and back at me. His eyes narrowed. He was thinking, I assumed, I hoped.

I felt excited and a bit scared. He might be an actual ghost. I grabbed a tree for support. Why he was here and why I am seeing him. These thoughts raced through my mind.

I looked at the Confederate, my hands up. I am sure I looked silly to him.

I said", Are you lost?"

The soldier smiled and spoke in a friendly, slow drawl.", No, but I believe you are."

The soldier was now a solid figure. He looked real, but I knew he wasn't. He was a REAL ghost, the one had seen in my imagination.

I could not contain myself; I whispered", Wow!'

I had met my ghost.

The Confederate soldier cocked his head to one side. "I don't know that word," he said.

I felt faint and sat down again on the ground. The soldier stepped forward, seemingly out of concern but careful not to touch me.

"Are you feeling poorly," the soldier asked.

I shook my head, looked into the soldier's eyes, and said:" What are you doing here?"

That question made the soldier smile again, and I realized I was stating the obvious. He belonged here. He was tied to this field. I got to my feet awkwardly. As I reached out for balance, I brushed the soldier's arm. An electric shock traveled up my arm and jolted my body.

I stepped back and shook my arm out while the soldier stood still. I had read about this phenomenon in my investigation. However, reading about it and feeling it were VERY different. I stepped back to avoid any more contact. By now, I was more annoyed than scared.

"I don't think you ought to do that," said the soldier.

I nodded and again asked,", Why are you here?"

The Confederate ghost answered," You must come back to that field."

He motioned for me to follow him. We walked back to the field. I stayed in the tree line, and the ghost walked out to the middle. The Confederate soldier turned, faced me, and stood in place.

The soldier said in a tearful voice", This is my grave. Others, too. Bobby, Little Bill, and Martin. It would help if you told those people. We want this place to be known." He stopped talking as if looking for the right words.

Then the soldier looked down at the ground and said," Little Bill, help me with the words."

The soldier seemed to get his answer, and he looked at me and said slowly, "Recognition.

'Yup, we want this place marked, recognition."

I asked," You and the others want this place recognized."

The soldier nodded.

I said, "Okay, Err, I mean, I will ask them to do it."

I immediately thought, what am I saying?

The thought must have registered on my face.

"Do I have your word?' he said.

I answered, Yes."

The soldier looked at me, smiled and saluted, and began to melt away. In a minute, he disappeared.

I yelled, "Wait! I want to know more." He smiled and shook his head as he faded. I just stood there, rooted in the ground. I alternated between shaking and smiling. Just a minute ago, I made a promise to keep to a ghost.

I slowly began to move again. I realized I had a job to do. I started to pace off from the tree to the spot of the graves. I wrote down the paces. I used my phone to get the coordinates. I wanted to say something, but nothing came to mind. I just crossed myself and whispered," I'll do it."

I left a marker of rocks at the site and returned to the car. I sat quietly, absorbing my experience. I grabbed a pad and wrote it all down. I had done it. I had seen a ghost. I was shaking, giddy, and accomplished.

At the hotel, I could not sleep. I replayed the experience.

"I should have asked questions."

Finally, I fell asleep.

I woke up and ate breakfast at the hotel. I stopped thinking of the experience and realized I had made a promise. I had work to do.

But I had to tell the park service to keep my promise. Would they believe me?

I drove to the park ranger station, and I was going to tell my story. I was sure they would think me whacko.

However, I introduced myself as a police detective and showed the ranger my badge. That gave me credibility. The ranger sat at his desk and listened. I repeated the story, and he started taking notes and asking questions.

I said, "I am sure he has seen many like me coming to report "seeing things."

Did he believe me?" I wondered. He had a constant smirk on his face.

He stood and led me to a park map. "Show me the location," he said.

He seemed to be giving me the benefit of the doubt. I pointed out the location using my phone. That impressed him.

I said, "I am telling the truth. It saw what I saw."

He looked at me for a long minute. The smirk disappeared. He started toward the back of the office. He stopped and turned and looked at me again. He said he was going to get his supervisor.

I heard talking, some laughter, then someone said, "Well, I'll be damned."

The ranger's supervisor waved me into his office.

"He introduced himself. I am Ranger Hancock, a park supervisor."

He had me repeat the story. He had me repeat to another ranger. They looked at each other. The supervisor said, "Sir, Do you know how many ghost stories we hear about the battlefield?" But I have to tell you, this one impresses me. We are all going to take a trip out to the field."

We stopped at the park map, and he looked at my coordinates.

We drove to the field in the four-by 4 in silence. The rangers decided if I saw something. I found the spot marked by the rock and repeated my story for at least the fifth time.

The supervisor stepped aside and discussed the circumstances with the two other rangers.

The supervisor indicated to the other ranger this had to be looked into.

The supervisor turned and said," I am calling for our team with ground-penetrating radar."

He described the radar as a "thing resembling a computer mounted on a walker."

Under the computer is a box with the radar in it. Its signal penetrates up to 15 feet. If there is anything down there, they will find it."

The Radar men arrived, and the machine. The supervisor explained the situation. They set it up in no time.

The new people took time to tape off the area in a grid. They took the radar and moved back]and forth over the marked-off area, similar to mowing grass.

Suddenly, the man with the radar stopped. He had a strong signal. Carefully, the team marked off the area where the signal was strongest. I almost jumped for joy.

"We will need government permission to dig'" said the supervisor.

"Do I get to know what you are looking for?"

A ranger said, "We are looking for a row of metal objects. They will show up in a straight line. Those are metal uniform buttons, and they mark a body."

He played the film back. I could see the button rows very clearly. The bodies were there.

The supervisor said, "I will have to consult Washington. They will decide what action, if any, will be done."

He continued," Even though you were on the property illegally, I appreciate this. It may come to some good. However, Do not come on this property again."

I said, "I understand," I said, "Goodbye."

I was dismissed from the field. A ranger drove me to the park ranger's office. I said goodbye and headed back to the hotel to pack.

I felt happy, believed, and relieved. My trip was a great success. I was now a ghost-seeing detective.

However, back home, my friends were still skeptical and sarcastic. They would smile as if they had heard a joke. Only my wife supported me.

Several months later, an official-looking National Park Service envelope arrived at my home.

In the letter was a picture of a marker in that same field. A newspaper article told of a ceremony held by the park service and the Daughters of the Confederacy.

The marker read," Here lies Our Brave Confederate Dead. May they rest in peace."

I would show those disbelieving friends the letter, picture, and newspaper article.

It felt so good. I had proof.

I had seen a ghost.

And more importantly, I kept my promise.

THE COURT MARTIAL FINISHED UP THE WITNESSES FOR THE PLAINTIFF

January 1865

The court-martial was held in a sterile, dimly lit room. The board finished up the witnesses for the plaintiff.

Major Robert Pulaski was being charged with everything from behavior unbecoming a Union officer to dispensing unauthorized drugs and, lastly, practicing what could be called witchcraft. The charge was brought against the Major by a group of Union doctors. Doctors he had worked with attacked his procedures, even though the work was successful.

As the court-martial officers left the room, the major sat alone, staring straight ahead unless the testimony was so unbelievable that he stared directly at the witness.

One witness, an ashen, thin man who said he was present when the major worked on wounded, called him a devil doctor. The Major smiled slightly, looked at the man, and then watched the board absorb the man's testimony. They seem to give this man no credibility.

Major Pulaski tried to introduce witnesses for his case. All were former patients of his, but all were enlisted men.

The court martial board tended to take officers' testimony over enlisted men's comments.

One doctor said, "Since these are enlisted men with no medical training, their testimony shouldn't be believed."

Major Pulaski's attorney stood up and said. "They are smart enough to know when they get better."

The board was unmoved.

Major Pulaski's chances of being acquitted as the board recessed for lunch were slim.

In effect, Major Pulaski treated many Union troops with remedies he had learned from the Apache. He served with the second cavalry in the Southwest before the civil war. There he knew what and how to use these medicines. The medicines were herbs, poultices, and moss from trees. Using these remedies, he was very successful in treating wounds. But the military doctor community was agitated and possibly jealous of his methods. Therefore, the effort to discredit Pulaski had grown. That is how we find the Major in court martial procedures.

The board went to lunch, and Major Pulaski was returned to his cell.

The court martial chairman had just been seated at his favorite table in the restaurant across from the court military area.

His lunch was interrupted by a soldier carrying a letter.

"This just arrived for you, General." said the soldier.

"Just put it with my hat and cloak. I will read it later. Thank you," replied the general.

The soldier hesitated and spoke again.

"The letter came through the lines, sir." Said the soldier.

The general looked up from his soup. He took the letter. The handwriting on the envelope looked familiar.

The general opened the letter, read it, and stopped. He stared at the soldier, exited his thoughts, and focused on the letter again.

He commanded the soldier to tell all of the officers of the court martial board to reassemble in 30 minutes.

He got up and, without eating, headed back to the court martial room.

In the closed session, the board members were shown the letter.

The general said, "I served with him. I know this to be his handwriting."

The door of the court martial room was opened to pour in the many spectators and the accused.

The general called the room to order.

"I have received some new evidence which the board feels should be introduced into the record."

The clerk of the court read the letter.

January 1865

To the court martial board, US Navy yard, Washington DC.

I have known Major Robert Pulaski for several years. I found him to be a respected doctor and a man of the highest character.

His methods, though unusual at times, were remarkably successful.

I recommend Major Pulaski to the board with the highest respect.

Your obedient servant

Robert E. Lee

Commanding the Army of Northern Virginia.

Half of the court martial board knew or served with Robert E. Lee.

His word was reverend. The court spectators were stunned. Major Pulaski sat there and smiled.

The board went into an adjoining room to deliberate.

Ten minutes later, the board returned.

The clerk announced that the officer was acquitted of all charges and free to go.

The court was dismissed.

Major Pulaski went on to serve in the army. He had a very distinguished career. Two years later, Major had lunch with Robert E. Lee. He thanked the general and, of course, prescribed a remedy for his wife's arthritis.

Years later, these remedies of the Native Americans became very well-known and used widely.

One Apache and Iroquois remedy was a very primitive form of penicillin.

BATTERY D
1ST N.Y.
LIGHT ARTILLERY
ARTILLERY BRIG
THIRD CORPS.

A BRIEF ENCOUNTER

The gunfire is over, but the smoke still lingers on Gettysburg National Battlefield Park. The crowd mingles with the re-enactors, asking questions, touching their rifles, and taking pictures.

Margaret Cobean Anderson sits on a stone wall watching the activity. She is particularly interested in a family crowded around the 1st New York Light Artillery monument. She thinks of her great-great-great-grandmother Mary, who was here with that unit on the last day of the battle over 140 years ago. She wonders what Mary would have thought of the re-enactment.

She could have told Margaret If it was anything like the actual battle.

Margaret had been told the story many times.

It would start the same every time.

The Cobeans could feel the day heating up even in the chilly, damp cellar. Since early this morning, they had not heard galloping horses, rumbling cannons, or gunfire. When the fighting started, the family huddled in the cellar for safety. As the battle wore on, they felt drained from the tension. With the morning came anger and resentment at being cooped up for over 24 hours in the cellar. They wanted to see the sun but were worried about what they might find outside. Finally, it was time for someone to climb out.

At 17, Mary was the tallest child in the family. She was mature for her age, quick-witted, and single-minded. She had taken over many family duties since her father joined the Union Army. Mary was itching to get out and see what was happening.

"Imagine! Confederate soldiers here in Gettysburg," Grandmother said for the seventh time.

Mary's mother told Mary to go to the well and bring water to the basement. Mary poked her blond head out of the basement, checked for anyone nearby, ran to the well, and returned in under five minutes. She said that there were few people in view. She had heard a noise, but it was faint; the soldiers were far off.

Mary had worried all night about her grandfather Jacob's gravestone. She wanted to check the marker as soon as possible. Since they heard, the battle yesterday had swirled around Evergreen Cemetery.

Mary asked her mom quietly, "I want to go check on Grandpa's marker, please."

She let that news be passed before she could run to Evergreen Cemetery and check on her grandfather's tombstone. Mary reminded her mother that the neighbor boy had called through the basement door last evening that fighting near the cemetery had moved away. Mary said, "It's miles away by now." They all stopped to listen. Grandma said she had not heard any gunfire in a couple of hours.

"Not," replied her mother.

"But the fight is up the ridge. I'll be fine," Mary said.

Mary could see that her mother was torn. Grandfather Jacob had been buried only a month before the battle.

"I'll be back in 30 minutes. Oh, please, please. I worried all night about Grandpa's stone," pleaded Mary.

Her mother knew Mary had been Grandpa Jacob's favorite.

Grandmother settled the argument by handing her a cloth and soapstone. "If there are any marks, these will get them off. Be careful, Sweetie," she said, turning a stern eye to the girl, then to her daughter.

Mary kissed both women and rushed out of the basement. She was in the field across Hanover Road, heading toward the cemetery before anyone realized she was out the cellar door.

It wasn't much more than a quarter-mile from Hanover Road through the field to Rock Creek. Mary followed it, passing several Union soldiers. They smiled and tipped their hats but did little else. She quickly made it to the main Federal lines. The soldiers were everywhere.

Some men were barking orders, some were trying to ignore those orders, and every size and type of equipment was everywhere. More than once, Mary bumped up against wagons or men hurrying somewhere or waiting for columns of blue-uniformed soldiers to pass. All the time, keeping her eyes on the Evergreen Cemetery gatehouse.

She arrived at the cemetery to find her grandfather's marker worse for wear. She looked at the gravestone and wept. The ground around it was covered with footprints and discarded equipment. A broken rifle was propped against the stone. Once white and shiny, the gravestone was covered with dirt; in the right corner was a bullet mark. Mary set to work cleaning, especially around the letters that spelled out Jacob Cobean. With the soapstone, the girl worked at the dent.

It was early afternoon, and the sun was so hot. Mary was soon sweating and feeling tired. She laid down for a break on the shady side of the marker. It was her first real rest in two days. She quickly fell asleep.

Mary awoke with a jump. She had felt the movement before she was completely awake. Men and horses go toward the South. That must be the front line.

It was time to go home. Mary pulled up her long dress to free her legs. She started to run and plowed headlong into a group of Union soldiers. A large, strongly built man with a black mustache hauled her up by her arms and laughed. "Here, here, where you off to, little sister?"

She dusted off, rearranged her skirt, stood tall, and answered, "I am headed home, sir."

"No sir, Little Sis, just sergeant. Sgt. Ziegler, at your service," he said with a mock salute. Mary smiled.

Sgt. Ziegler said there would be no going anywhere right at present. "Too much development going on. The lines are set; everyone seems to be waiting for something to happen. We mize well sit a spell."

Mary smiled, relaxed, and thought she would like this big man. He and his friend Alfee invited Mary to the mess tent for coffee and biscuits.

While eating, Mary quickly made friends with the two men. Both soldiers were 1st New York Light Artillery, Battery B. They had thick accents, and that made everything they said sound funny. Sgt. Ziegler and Alfee came from New York's west side. They told her of their home, family, food, and fun. Sgt. Ziegler talked of the battle and how they had moved around Gettysburg. They liked the Pennsylvania countryside, but it sure was hot. Mary laughed at their stories until her side hurt. Alfie, with his Dutch New York accent, could never quite say Cobean. Mary began to feel like a sister to the two. Mary learned that Alfee was called "Shorty" because, looking at him, the nickname just sounded right. She also knew that no one expected much action on this side of the field. The battle down the line had ended about noon. Both sides had decided to rest.

Since it was quiet and expected to stay that way, Sgt, Ziegler, and Shorty invited Mary to see their battery. To hear the two tell it, the 1st New York Light Artillery, Battery B, was the best battery in the army. They were very proud of their unit and wanted to show it off.

It was about 3:00 pm on July 3. Suddenly, Mary heard cannon fire. Shorty assured her that it would hit the east of their unit. He said, "We are not in the line of shot. "The three quickly marched a half-mile across Taneytown Pike. Confederate cannons were still firing beyond their position.

Mary and the two soldiers came upon the battery of four brass canons. The battery was set up 50 yards in front of a stone wall. Sgt. Ziegler pointed to a tree line through the summer haze and said, "You'll find scores of rebels among those trees!"

"So close!" said Mary.

Mary was introduced to some of the soldiers handling the battery. She smiled as they talked but could not understand much of what they said. Their accents were thicker than Ziegler's. Some of the men appeared to be new to America. Their German was better than their English.

Sgt. Ziegler escorted Mary over to an officer. He saluted and introduced her to Capt. Rorty, the battery commander. Capt. Rorty was very handsome in his blue cap and long hair. He smiled at Mary and started to tell Ziegler it was time to get the little girl back. But he stopped mid-sentence. Capt. Rorty was looking in the direction of the woods. He continued to look toward the trees. Something was coming.

All the Union troops strained to see through the summer haze. Suddenly, the rebels were streaming out of the distant tree line. Mary could see flags and hear a band playing as a parade.

Rorty looked through his sight glasses. He drew a breath and whispered, "Oh God, they are dressing ranks."

As if the whole line heard Capt. Rorty, a collective gasp came from all around. Mary realized that parade, that terrible parade, was coming at them. The Union cannons—indeed, the whole Union battle line—stood spellbound at the sight of the Confederate advance.

Suddenly everybody moved at once. Ziegler grabbed Mary's hand and rushed her to a spot about 50 yards behind the guns. He left her behind a small wagon.

"Stay here, Little Sister, stay here! You are just as safe here as anywhere!" she heard him say as he returned to his guns.

In the beginning, Mary just heard men running and music playing. She saw a horse break free. But it seemed like a powerful thunderstorm was starting and moving in on her. Soon she could hear nothing but the blast of thunder, sharp and close. The violence of it seemed to suck the air out of her. She had trouble breathing. The ground quaked so hard it caused her nose to bleed. She could see but not hear. The sound pushed her to the ground. Things hit the wagon, and dirt spurted up from her right hand. Mary was aware of men near her. The sound of the overwhelming storm seemed almost to crush her. Everything started to blur....

She blinked awake as the storm appeared to blow itself out. The thunder was lessening and passing suddenly, as with a summer storm. No more music. No more solitary shouts. The booming faded.

Mary was so scared that she shook. Wherever she looked up, there were injured men. They asked for her help by reaching hands. Slowly, she moved toward them. Soon Mary recognized Shorty. She moved to his side. He gave her a sad little smile and lay down. Tearing her petticoat, she placed a piece over the wound on his leg.

More help arrived to help the wounded. An officer directed Mary to help as she could. She moved from one wounded man to another, vomiting in between from the sight of the carnage. Finally, more medical staff arrived, and Mary moved back to Shorty and asked, "Where is the sergeant?"

Shorty pointed toward the cannons. Mary had to see if Sgt. Ziegler was all right.

She ran toward the guns. Mary was surprised by the cheering. She slowed to try to make out the words. Off to her right were men moving rebel prisoners toward the rear. Mary slowly approached the stone wall, stopped, and looked to the other side of the wall. She saw piles of clothing covering the field. It took a couple of minutes to realize these were bodies.

The field was covered with bodies, equipment, and smoke. The heat radiated off the ground, causing a haze. It was quiet across the stone wall, contrasted with the noise around her. Her legs shook as she moved toward the wall.

With dirt on her face and trailing part of her torn dress, Mary hesitantly walked into the 1st New York Light Artillery. She felt heaviness and dread. Four guns had been Battery B. Now only two were upright. One gun was completely turned over. She tried to keep her eyes high to avoid seeing the bodies. She knew she had to look.

She realized that the long blue coat by the overturned gun covered Capt. Rorty. She recognized the blue cape over his face. She bent down, uncertain of what she would do.

All of a sudden, Mary heard her name. She stood up and looked around. Her name came again, with an "Over here, Sister!"

She saw Ziegler had crossed the stone wall. He was bending by what appeared to be a pile of clothes, mouthing words. "Get me some water, Little Sis," he called as he stood up.

Mary returned with a canteen and handed it to Ziegler. He lifted not a man but a boy and gave him a drink.

The boy appeared to be just a little older than Mary. He had blond, sweaty hair and a dirty but handsome face. He gulped and turned and smiled at both. The soldier mouthed more words, but Mary did not understand. Mary noticed a piece of cloth pinned to the boy's coat lapel.

She bent her head toward him and read, "J. Marshall, 11 VA. "Mary knew soldiers going into battle often marked a paper and pinned it to their clothing. She smiled at him and helped Zeigler give him some more water. The boy also smiled but said nothing.

Ziegler slowly pulled the canteen away and gently laid the boy down. Ziegler reached down and covered his face with his grey jacket. "He's gone, Little Sister!"

"So quick. He was smiling at me. Oh, God." Ziegler stepped over and hugged her.

Tears filled her eyes. She whispered a prayer.

The sergeant and the girl stood and looked over the field. Piles of clothing were everywhere, with arms and legs sticking out of them.

They were talking to the men at the battery just a short time ago. Roughly two hours had passed. But right here, right now, time appeared to stall and freeze. The field smelled of gunpowder, and something sweetly sickening that Ziegler said was the scent of death.

The two sat on the wall in silence. Together they got up and turned toward the battery. Both appeared to be in a trance, maybe in shock.

"Let's go, Little Sis!" Ziegler said as he held her shoulders.

The new commanding officer, Lt. Rogers, stood over Capt. Rorty's body is obviously in shock. Ziegler asked if he could take Mary back to her home. The lieutenant nodded without really hearing Ziegler. All the men seemed to move in slow motion. Some were sitting on the ground, staring at nothing.

Ziegler walked Mary back to Shorty to check on him. Shorty was sleeping by one of the caissons. Ziegler covered him with a blanket. They turned toward Gettysburg.

Her mother's and grandmother's worry melted into relief as they ran to meet Ziegler and Mary. They hugged Sgt. Ziegler asked to come to sit on their porch. They gave him excellent cider. There were no questions for the two survivors. All four just sat quietly, looking across Hanover Road into the smoke.

As evening approached, Mary stood on her porch to watch Ziegler walk into the smoke covering the town. Ziegler waved back, then turned away. Mary sat on the front step and stared after him for a long time. The next day, Mary alternated between sleeping and crying.

It was over a week before people began to know Mary's story. She was a heroine. This 17-year-old girl had stood among the guns at Gettysburg. But the 17-year-old cared little for her fame. She avoided it and only once attended a parade during the first veteran reunion. Only Ziegler came back. He and Shorty had opened a printing company, and Shorty had stayed to mind the business. Mary and Ziegler were together for about five hours. They both looked the same. Only their eyes said they were different.

Ziegler and Mary Cobean took the time that day to talk and meet other veterans. Late in the afternoon, the two walked to the wall, sat on it, and remembered the young man, J Williams, 11 VA, who had died in front of Battery B, 1st New York Light Artillery. The field was so different. Gone were the dead, the destruction and the smoke, and in their place, green lawn, bright sunlight, and quiet cannons as monuments.

And that had been the story told in Margaret's family.

Of course, the battlefield is much changed—a national park. Thousands of people come here daily, some to enjoy history, some to reflect, and all to reverence this place.

Margaret Cobean Anderson, retired teacher, and family historian, works at the park's visitor's center. It seems to keep her close to the Mary Cobean of 1863. She has spent much of her time researching her ancestor. Today, especially, she remembers Mary. The date is July 3, 2003.

One hundred forty years ago, not more than 300 yards from the visitors' center, her ancestor hid behind a caisson. Margaret's thoughts of Mary keep popping into her head. It was close to the exact time the battle ended. She is lost in that thought as she places brochures on a rack.

Movement catches her eye. The doors at the main entrance start to open but then close. She watches this happen again. Margaret goes to the big wooden doors and pulls. The doors are heavy, and she has to use both hands. To her surprise, an elderly woman with a walker is stuck in the door. Mary remembers the woman was at the re-enactment; they had talked briefly. She liked the sound of the woman's Southern accent.

"Let's try to pull," says Margaret.

The woman nods, and together they push and pull. But now, the door is stuck.

A large man arrives and puts his arm against the door. "I think I can get it free. You step back," he says to Mary.

Suddenly, Margaret feels a tingle and a breeze. She shivers, and, to her astonishment, the large man looks startled too. Something has passed between them. It gave her goosebumps. But as quickly as it came, it passed. They were strangers, yet she seemed to know this man.

The man pushes the door open enough to free the woman.

The door opens, and the frail woman in the walker moves through the doorway. The look on the woman's face says she, too, had felt that sensation. It was a quizzical expression.

However, she looks like she will collapse; she's slumped on her walker. Margaret and the man quickly move her to a bench near the doors. The man kneels beside the woman to comfort her.

"Please, could I have some water?" the woman whispers.

"Sure, lady," says the man.

Margaret brings him a plastic cup, and he goes to the water fountain.

The woman drinks and seems to rally. She smiles at them. "That was excellent. May I have another?" the woman says in a soft Southern accent.

Margaret goes for more water. As the woman drinks, Margaret introduces herself, and the woman does the same. "I am Florence Matthews, from Abington, Virginia," she says.

The big man doffs his New York ball cap. "Hi. I'm Bob Roush, from New York City," he says proudly.

They huddle around the woman on the bench until it becomes clear she's breathing better. They talked about the re-enactment.

Bob starts to look for his family. Then he turns with a peculiar look and says, "Do I know you?"

The woman with the walker says, "No, I'm not from here."

Margaret listens very intently. The scene is familiar. But how can that be?

Margaret waits for Florence's family to find her. The family came in and ran up to the bench, all talking at once. After Margaret explains what happened, she touches Florence's shoulder and turns to leave. Bob tips his ball cap and excuses himself to find his family.

Florence calls softly after both, "Thank you for your kindness."

Margaret smiles, nods, and walks back to the desk.

She thought, what was that sensation that passed through her?

She was sure the big man and the elderly felt something too.

Of course, we know who Margaret is: Mary Cobean's descendent. And Bob from New York is the great-great-grandson of Robert Ziegler, Sergeant, Battery B, 1st New York Light Artillery. Florence is a descendant of the boy who died in Ziegler's arms. Mary and Ziegler had given him water. His grave marker at Gettysburg reads J. Williams, 11th Virginia Infantry.

Why did Florence and Bob decide to journey to the National Park on this day? Why did they arrive at this particular moment? Maybe because this is Florence's last year at the visitors center. It's Bob's first. He always wanted to come to see where his great-great-great-grandfather fought. Margaret…well, she had to be here to complete the scene.

There could be another answer. But there are twists of time when a scene is recreated with a new but familiar cast, and just the ending has changed.

THE MAGICAL SHOP OF
LOST AND FOUND

As I researched stories for the book on the Civil War, "The Civil War with a Twist," I came across a story shaded in myth and hearsay. I never could pinpoint a reliable source, but the rumors persisted, much repeated, containing the same descriptions. As with all folktales, the story was passed on by mouth. Many believe it is just a tall tale.

The most extraordinary fact was the name, the Magical Shop of Lost and Found. There, you could find almost anything you lost: items, feelings, or all things necessary.

Legend has it that the shop was located in Baltimore, Maryland, between 1850 and 1869. It is told to seek out a particular group of women of color to find it. These women live near the central market, accepting their roles as gatekeepers. The women would deem your need worthy of a trip to the shop. They wear blue-green scarves or hats to be easily identified. One of the women would give you written directions to navigate the warren of back alleys. As you follow the path to the shop, you will see these written directions disappear from the page. It ensures that your journey is a one-time walk. You leave the shop at the end of the meeting, finding yourself not in the alley but on a busy thoroughfare or at the docks. The shop has disappeared.

The bright red door can be recognized from a block away. There is no doorknob. The door opens inwards. A slit at eye level will open after you knock four times and announce your name. You were expected, it seems. You will never know how the Keeper knew you were coming.

The Keeper is a giant who walks with a stoop. He wears thick glasses. His voice is a cross between a whisper and a growl. He knows the exact spot of your item. He moves silently, but you step on the wood floor, creaking and groaning under your feet. He has an aura that people never forget. It is one of extreme age, wisdom, and power.

Once inside, you will find yourself in a massive warehouse, a maze of winding aisles, shelves, and drawers crammed with items and containers. There are mysterious recesses and spaces between the shelves. A half-light comes through the shutters, the only relief from the dusty darkness. The shop should be gloomy, but it has enough light to see.

Drawers are marked in the beautiful bold script as if penned long ago by silent monks. You will be directed down the central aisle and then to a particular row to your lost "something."

I wanted to know more about this Magic Shop of Lost and Found. So, I headed for the Library of Congress in DC. It was an exciting story. I asked at the desk. The librarian was startled, and after he regained his senses, he said to go to the back of the room; I will find someone to help.

I found elevators at the back of the massive main reading room. A young woman walked up and pushed a button to open the doors. I walked in, and she reached in and hit a floor button. The doors closed, and I was alone. The elevator took a long time to travel to the right floor.

Suddenly the doors opened to a dark and somewhat creepy floor. I stepped off. The door closed so quickly. I just pulled my briefcase out.

I asked if anyone was there, but no one came. I said it louder; no one came. Just as I was about to scream, a voice from somewhere on the floor answered, "Coming."

A dapper man with a suit and tie greeted me.

"What can I do for you?"

I asked for information about The Magical Shop of Lost and Found.

He stepped back and asked how I had heard of such a place. I took my notes and briefly read what I had in the shop.

He turned and took me to a desk, switched on the light, and left. I pulled out my recorder, paper, and pen.

He returned with four leather-bound journals, telling me immediately not to use the recorder.

He sat across from me and started telling me about the journals.

"These are the remembrances of some of the Magical Shop of Lost and Found keepers. They are exceptional. You may read them here and take WRITTEN NOTES. Neither journals nor any part of the journal may leave this floor. And to answer your first question, you cannot take a picture of them."

I said, Is it against library policy?" "No, they will not show up.

"What" He said to take out my phone and snap a picture.

I did, and there was the table and the light but no journal. I tried twice, but no journal appeared on the phone camera.

I started to realize this search was going to be something special.

He smiled and said the library closes at 5 pm. I was so excited; I was shaking. I got right to work. The journals were well-written but with pieces that needed to be included.

They told the stories of people who had used the Magical Shop of the Lost and Found.

I picked 4 of the tales. I will give them to you.

1

A Union Army soldier was sent home due to his wife's passing. He arrived in Baltimore to find that his wife had been buried just days before. He went through her belongings but could not find her most prized possession: the oversized sweater she wore in the winter. It was blue and gold with a wide green stripe across the chest. He hunted high and low, but no sweater. He asked around the neighborhood. Finally, he was directed to the dock area by a neighbor, known to be a person of special knowledge.

He was to ask for a particular woman wearing a blue and green scarf. It was late in the afternoon when he found her. He told his story. The story was deemed deserving. He received the written directions to the shop.

The soldier was instructed to hold the writing over a candle. The directions would appear, and that night, they did.

He started early on a frosty morning but quickly became lost. He got to a particular spot, then doubled back when he found out the directions for that stage of the journey had disappeared.

He began to ask people about a red door. Hearing of his pleas, another woman of color walked him to the alley leading to the red door. Then she quickly walked away.

He knocked. The eye slit opened. The Keeper asked his name, and the door flew open. The Keeper stepped back to let him pass.

Before the soldier could tell the Keeper what he was looking for.

"Go down three rows, turn right, and look for the drawer marked Special Garments," the Keeper told him. The soldier was amazed and cautiously walked toward row three. He could not help but look back. The Keeper had disappeared.

The soldier found the sweater and put it on. It felt as if his wife was hugging him through the beautiful blue and gold sweater with the wide green stripe.

He turned to find the Keeper standing right behind him.

The soldier said, "Sorry, I did not hear you coming."

The Keeper smiled, touched a sweater sleeve, and said, "No one ever does. I can see why this is so precious to you."

He continued, "You have found your Lost. "

The old soldier was led to the door. He said goodbye, exited the shop, and found himself standing on a Baltimore main street. The shop, the ivy half covering the red door, and the wall were gone.

Bewildered but happy, he headed home. He had been instructed to tell no one about the shop. It was a small price to pay for his wife's sweater, memory, and love.

2

A young John Clark lived in Baltimore and was being sent back to his cavalry unit. The year was 1864. His parents were so proud of John. They gave him a beautiful new Navy Colt revolver that later became the envy of his unit. The parents said the pistol would bring him home safely. The young trooper cleaned the gun several times. During the last cleaning, he lost a part. The part, that was crucial to the weapon, was the firing pin.

He could not tell his father. He was leaving in three days and would surely be in action. The housemaid found him tearing his room up, looking for the revolver piece, John was her favorite. He would go to the market with her and help her carry packages from time to time. The following day, she took John with her. He was sure she could help.

The maid asked around until they were face to face with a woman of color with a blue-green hat. The maid left the soldier with the lady of color.

She took John to the middle of the city and gave the soldier written directions to the Magical Shop of Lost and Found. With the rules came a warning to show these to no one.

Following the directions, the young cavalryman found himself standing in front of the red door. The eye slit opened. The Keeper would not open the door. He told the soldier to come back when called.

Upset and frustrated, the cavalry trooper hit the door with his hand. The slit closed. The door faded into the stone wall, and the soldier turned around, finding himself standing at the dockside. Frightened, he ran back to his house.

He did not dare tell his family about the missing part and placed the pistol in a saddle holster his brother made especially for John. The expensive pistol remained in the saddle holster. However, the young soldier had purchased a cheap colt for the coming fight.

Four weeks later, the young soldier's unit was involved in heavy fighting at Yellow Tavern. The battle ebbed and flowed around the tavern. As the day continued, the war changed from rushes at each side to individual hand-to-hand combat. As evening came, the sides began to break off the engagement. The young Union cavalryman was still locked in a struggle with a Rebel cavalryman. They wrestled while on horseback. The rebel pushed the Union cavalryman almost off his horse.

As John Clark righted himself, the rebel spotted the handle of the Colt. He pulled it out of the holster, pointed it at the Union cavalryman, and yelled, "Goodbye, Yank." He cocked the gun and pulled the trigger. The gun did not fire. The rebel cocked and pulled the trigger again. John Clark leaned over his saddle, knocked the gun out of the Rebel's hand, and punched the Confederate a heavy blow.

The rebel hanging over his saddle rode away. The battle started to clear out, and the participants rode away. As the battle closed, few were left on the field. The Union cavalryman rode back to where he thought the gun had dropped. After an hour of searching, he caught a glimpse of the Colt pistol. He dismounted and retrieved his pistol. He stood there, holding the gun, shaking. Slowly he mounted and rode to join his unit.

While on leave, the young man told the family of the gun's misfiring and how it had saved his life.

The housemaid called the young soldier into the kitchen one morning, and the same lady of color handed him a note. He could now return for his lost part.

The trooper smiled and declined. "I learned more from the part being missing!" The lady in the blue, green hat smiled. Nodded and said, "Just so."

The colt was handed down through the family. The Clark family of Baltimore, Maryland, still has the Colt pistol and tells the story.

3

The fame and myth of the Magical Shop of Lost and Found soon would be known to a Confederate lieutenant named George Dixon. The lieutenant carried a gold coin in his chest pocket. At the battle of Shiloh, the coin stopped a direct hit. After the fighting, he sanded down the unmarked side and engraved the words, My Life Preserver. He was his talisman; he took it with him everywhere.

After the battle, he was called to his hometown of Charleston, South Carolina. Officers in the Confederate Navy interviewed him. After some leave, he would be assigned a special, secret mission. While at home with his family, somehow, Dixon lost his lucky gold coin during a party at a friend's house. He was very depressed. His wife had never seen him so upset. She checked with her friends to see if anyone had seen the coin. The next day a striking woman of color appeared and told him about the Magical Shop of Lost and Found. However, It was in Baltimore beyond the Union lines. Since he felt all luck had left. A feeling of doom came over him, and this may well be the only way to get the coin. He would risk the danger of going through Union lines to Baltimore. The city was full of Confederate sympathizers. These people would secret him into a hotel and escort him around Baltimore.

After three days of travel, mostly at night and along back roads, he arrived in Baltimore.

George woke early and headed to the market. Within an hour, he met a striking woman of color. As foretold, She had a blue-green sash around her waist. She listened to his story and told him to return to his hotel. He was puzzled, but the woman assured him it would be all right.

Armed with the instructions left for him at the hotel desk, he started to find The Magical Shop of Lost and Found the next day. After a long and winding route, he knocked on the red door. The eye slit revealed understanding eyes.

The lieutenant introduced himself. The Keeper said he had been told of his coming.

"How," asked Lt. Dixon.

"Oh, our ways are never explained. They just are. Come this way; I know exactly where you should look." Said the Keeper.

The lieutenant was directed down an aisle to a drawer labeled Lucky Coins. He shifted through the coins. The coin was there. He was safe again. His good luck would continue as long as he had the coin.

The Keeper touched his arm as the lieutenant started to leave through the red door. He said, "The coin may not always work. It may be your time. Be prepared. Luck can be a will-of-wisp." Before the lieutenant could ask what the Keeper meant, the door closed, and he was on the street near his Confederate-friendly hotel.

That night, Lieut. Dixon started his way through Union lines to Charleston, South Carolina. After returning home, he was called to the Confederate Navy headquarters and his new adventure. But the Keeper's words echoed in his head, but the lieutenant convinced himself that the man was philosophizing.

Lieut. Dixon, armed with his lucky coin, was about to make history.

Dixon was transferred to the Confederate Navy and was the commander of the Confederate secret weapon, a submersible. The submersible was considered a real chance to break the Union Blockade of Southern ports. An explosive attached at the end of an 18' boom would be on the front of the submersible. The bomb would be stuck to the hull of a Union ship using pitch and gum. The submersible would pull away, and the detonator would explode the charge; it was an ingenious idea, but the submersible had to work. After explaining the plan, his commander told him, "The new submersible called the Hunley. It was to be commanded by Captain Dixon. The Navy officers made Dixon aware this was the seventh try to make submersibles work.

Lieutenant now Captain Dixon chooses 7 for his school and army friends. They thought this was an adventure until the hard work of turning the propeller hit them.

After many trials, the Hunley was deemed ready. Dixon said goodbye to his wife and headed to the shore of Charleston Bay. His lucky coin was in his pocket. With this, he felt confident the Hunley would work. The Hunley set out to the Union blockade line on a night with a full moon and a glass sea. If the mission was successful and the ship escaped, it would show a blue light from its forward hatch. The shore party would light a blue light to guide the Hunley back to base.

It took an hour to get to the first Union battleship.

The soldiers on shore saw the explosion. The Battleship rose out of the water. It quickly sank within minutes; The Hunley flashed a blue light. After repeated signals from the shore,the land party stopped. The Hunley never returned. Researchers figured out that the shock waves from the explosion may have killed Dixon and his crew. But many years of searching had not revealed the famous Confederate submersible.

For 140 years, they searched for the Hunley. Several Likely wrecks were uncovered, but none were the real Hunley. In 2005, another wreckage was found intact. Once brought to the surface and placed in a saltwater bath, they started the grisly task of removing the human remains. They still were not convinced this was the real submersible.

An archeologist who had researched the Hunley knew how to get this proof arrived at the North Charleston site. They found their proof at the bottom of the boat when it was cleared of debris. As she shifted thru the debris, she found a gold coin marked My Life Preserver. George Dixon had commanded the submersible into history.

Suppose you travel to North Charleston to the Hunley Museum. You will see the Hunley. Lt. George Dixon's lucky coin is in the middle of an artifact display table. It may cause you to wonder about the Magical Shop of Lost and Found's reality.

But the stories continue.

4

The war was over. Peace was at hand. Washington, DC, was jubilant. The young Union officer had tickets to "the play" of Our American Cousin. But the real reason for taking a group of ladies to the play was at the intermission, he planned to propose to his fiancé.

In addition to tickets for himself and his fiancé, he had bought tickets for his mother and her mother. Then, he lost his ticket. The play was sold out. He was in a stew. Then, a ray of hope.

A neighbor who grew up in the magic tradition knew a particular woman who might help. The neighbor sent him to Baltimore.

A woman of color in a blue-green turban at the Baltimore market listened to the officer's story. She was a romantic. She said she would help. She told him about the Magical Shop of Lost and Found. He was given directions and the warning that they would dissolve as he went along on his way.

He was precise in following the directions, and within 30 minutes, he was standing in front of the red door.

The eye slit opened; the door opened. The Keeper greeted the officer and escorted him to a far row. The officer went alone to find the drawer marked Tickets. The happy soldier found the lost ticket and almost skipped back to the Keeper.

"Young man," said the Keeper. "Things do not always come complete with finding your lost item. This ticket may take you to more than you are a bargain for. But good luck."

The officer had not a care in the world. Dressed in his best uniform, with a ring in his pocket and a ticket in his hand, the officer strolled into Ford's Theatre with his party. The theater was decked out in patriotic banners. The president was going to attend the play.

The group arrived at their floor seats and settled. Then, Mr. Lincoln and his entourage arrived. There were applause and cheers. Finally, the audience settled into their seats.

The play was in the second act; it was wonderful, then a gunshot interrupted the night. It sounded very close. The crowd could smell the gunpowder. The shot was followed by a crazed man standing and yelling from the stage. There were screams, and all eyes turned to the president's box. The four stood and watched the president carried from the theater. They waited with many others. The news was finally called out from the house across from Ford's Theater. Lincoln had died. And the night meant to be such a happy memorable occasion would be memorable for the tragedy.

John Hopkins and Mary Lombardo did become engaged but much later. They did not want that anniversary to be remembered as the date they witnessed the assassination of Abraham Lincoln. Mary kept the tickets in her bible, looked at them rarely, but remembered everything.

Four stories awash in myth, good intentions, luck, and unexpected results. I've gone to Baltimore and searched for that red door; I found one, but it was a bar.

It seems that new accounts of the Magical Shop of Lost and Found did not end; it moved to another place. Numerous cities have been mentioned in the research.

Even though I do not need to search for a lost item, I'll keep the story alive regarding the "magical shop of lost and found."

Even if it is just a legend, and these stories are just stories. The idea of The Magical Shop of Lost and Found is grand.

GETTYSBURG

It started as a quiet evening at the Pennsylvania National Guard camp. The Guard was performing its required two weeks of field training exercises. The units began to move into an area next to Gettysburg National Park. As the Guardsmen put the camp together, a most peculiar storm moved into the area. It grew in intensity and, with it, a feeling that something strange was coming. The clouds turned ugly. They swirled and produced a dark purple. There was lightning, as Few had seen such a storm. The lightning and the gusts of wind blew heavily across the camp. The storm was fast-moving, knocking down tents, blowing supplies all over the field, and leaving the camp a shambles. The puzzling storm had shocked and visibly shaken the troops. It took hours to reset the camp in almost total silence among the Guardsmen. They were nearly shocked as much as surprised by the storm by its intensity.

The following morning, many of the Guardsmen complained of restless sleep. The talk of the camp was the clouds and how odd they looked. In contrast, the morning was bright and fresh, and all seemed normal. But the Guardsmen could not predict what they would experience with the first patrol exercise.

Tango 5 patrol consisting of four Guardsmen, left camp on its pre-designed route. The four paid more attention to the storm than where they were headed.

"It was not normal, I tell you," said the sergeant. "We never have a storm like that," said the driver.

The Humvee turned a sharp corner on the wooded road and almost drove over three Civil War re-enactors. The vehicle braked hard, and the Guardsmen just looked at the three, dressed in Confederate uniforms. They look so authentic, with dirty uniforms, slouched hats, and muskets. They looked bedraggled and tired and completely surprised by the Humvee. They were dis-believing as they held their muskets at the ready. One re-enactor played his role by pointing his weapon at the Humvee.

The Guardsmen just sat and stared. Finally, the sergeant said," Hey, you guys look incredible. But I have to tell you this is a restricted area."

He stepped out of the vehicle, continuing to talk, "How did you get here in the first place."

All of the re-enactors raised their weapons.

"Whoa, dudes. This is not funny," said Sergeant Jacobs as he cautiously walked toward the re-enactors with his hands up.

"I am going to ask you for some ID. And then you will have to leave this area."

Suddenly one of the re-enactors shouldered his musket and fired. It knocked Sergeant Jacobs off his feet. Two of the Guardsmen ran to his aid. The remaining Guardsmen moved to the machine gun. He cocked it and pointed it in the direction of the re-enactors.

As the two helped Jacobs to his feet, one yelled, "What is wrong with you people? As Sergeant Jacobs regained his breath, he cussed, threw off his helmet, and was ready to punch someone as he moved toward the re-enactors.

Seeing the sergeant rise, two of the re-enactors fled. The one, who fired the shot, fainted on the spot.

The driver returned to the Humvee and called on the radio, "This is Tango 5; we have an emergency; get someone here quick. Our position is two miles outside the camp.

Guardsmen Roberts and Sulley attended to the re-enactor. They brought him around and gave him a drink. The sergeant collapsed onto the ground. Wilks removed Jacob's protective vest and looked at the giant bruise on his chest.

"You are going to be sore for days, Sarge," said Wilks.

As they attended to the re-enactor and the sergeant, a group of re-enactors returned. Sulley jumped into the Humvee and readied the machine gun.

"You know something is not correct. These re-enactors look real. Do any of you guys get that idea? Said Wilks.

Roberts and Sully looked at Wilks as if he was crazy.

Everyone jumped as a second Humvee arrived with a guard officer. Several more re-enactors came with a brilliant-looking Confederate officer.

The Guard officer huddled with his men. They explained what had happened. Jacobs showed the officer his bruise. The Guard officer turned to confront the re-enactors.

The Guard officer was an unusual sight; John Browning, dressed in rumpled camouflaged battle gear, and the re-enactor officer dressed for a ball in a pressed uniform with shiny brass buttons.

"What the hell is going on?" demanded the guard captain. "I am going to ask for your weapons, and someone may go to jail."

The re-enactor officer bristled, "Just who are you all." He spoke with a thick Southern accent.

Captain Browning put his hands on his hip and, in a loud voice, said," For your information, we are part of the 4th Mechanized Cavalry, Pennsylvania National Guard. You are in a restricted area and have just shot one of my men."

"Explain your Self" The re-enactors raised their muskets at the name Pennsylvania, and the Guardsmen raised their weapons.

"Whoa," said Browning, and he moved between the groups and waved his arms for all to lower their weapons.

Both sides did as requested. Both groups seemed to calm down.

The Guard officer and the re-enactor officer walked to a spot away from the two groups. The National Guard officer played along with the re-enactors. He saluted the Confederate officer and introduced himself.

"Captain John Browning "

In return, the re-enactor officer saluted, "Captain Brett Mosser, 14th Virginia Infantry, at your service."

Captain Browning repeated that the group was restricted and would have to leave.

"I beg your pardon. Do you know who we are?" asked Captain Mosser.

"Er, yes, you are re-enactors," answered the Guard Officer.

Captain Mosser's face turned red, "actors, actors, he stammered," I assure you, sir, we are not some fancy pants actors."

Captain Browning was taken back and said, "Well, yes, I understand. But you will have to move out of this area."

The re-enactor officer stepped back, and the re-enactor soldiers, who had been listening., raised their muskets. The Guardsmen stepped behind the Humvee and knelt in firing position.

The tense moment was broken by Sergeant Jacobs storming back between two groups and cussing before he stopped to realize where he was.

The re-enactors stood in stunned silence. The Guardsmen turned Jacobs around and walked to the Humvee. Wilks and Sulley started to laugh.

"It ain't funny," cussed Jacobs.

"It's a little bit funny," said Sulley.

The re-enactor, who fired the shot, paled and asked in astonishment, "How could ye be alive?"

The re-enactor soldiers, wide-eyed and dumbfounded, backed away as if confronted by a ghost.

Jacobs was guided to behind the vehicle.

Wilks said, "Sir, I called for backup, and none other than General Abrams is on his way."

Captain Browning answered, "Oh, Brother!" He turned toward the re-enactor officer and said, "Captain Mosser, you understand we will have to take your man into custody."

Again, the guns were raised by both sides.

Browning yelled in frustration, "Now hold up. Can you show some ID"? The re-enactors looked at each, and one said, "What is this ID you keep talking about?" The Guard Officer said," Where are you from?" The re-enactors responded in unison, "Virginia."

It was apparent that the re-enactors would play this to the end. Both groups backed up further apart. After talking to his men, the re-enactor officer left. Both groups eyed each other, but no one raised weapons.

Moments later, Captain Mosser returned with a tall, burly distinguished officer. He had a long beard. His dress was perfect. The officer looked as if he had walked out of a movie.

"Wow." Said a Guardsman.

Captain Browning said, "He looks like he just walked out of a history book."

Wilks said, "This guy is somebody. We need our own ranker."

With that remark, Browning told Wilks to call on the radio again.

The re-enactors followed the new impressive officer back toward the Humvee.

"Here we go again," said Captain Browning as he walked up to meet the group. The Captain saluted the officer and repeated his name and unit.

The newly arrived officer returned the salute and asked, "How did you people come to be in this place?" "Sir, we are conducting summer maneuvers," Captain Browning answered back.

Just as the re-enactor officer started to talk, he was interrupted by the sound of a helicopter. The re-enactors looked up at the sky and ran, terrified, into the nearby woods. Only the bearded officer held his spot.

The helicopter landed behind the woods, but everyone felt the wind wash over them.

"What in tarnation was that?" shouted the re-enactor officer. He did not show if he was scared, but his face showed that he knew something strange was happening.

The other re-enactors slowly emerged from the woods. They huddled around their officer for comfort.

Both groups waited and watched. Within minutes, General Josh Abrams appeared and was briefed by Browning. The sergeant showed the general his bruise and pointed at the re-enactors. General Abrams spun around and walked straight toward the re-enactors.

General Abrams is tall, grey-haired, and roughly handsome. He likes to laugh, but in this case, he showed he was not ready for foolishness.

As Abrams walked, he thought, "That guy sure looks the part."

The two men saluted and began to take the measure of each other. Neither side could hear what they were saying, but the generals' stern looks did not rest well with either side.

As the generals talked, Abrams's aide, Captain Mauger, secretly took a picture of the re-enactor general with his phone. He googled the re-enactors picture.

"No way, "The general's aide said as he gazed at his phone. His mouth dropped open, and he ran toward the two generals.

"Excuse me, general, can I see you a minute," he shouted.

Both generals looked at him.

"Excuse me, sir, I meant my general," he pointed to Abrams.

General Abrams followed him to the rear of the Humvee. Both Guard officers looked at the phone at each other and toward the re-enactor general, then back to the phone.

The aide said," I had a hunch when I saw him."

"NO way' said Abrams. "Way," laughed the aide.

The two Guard officers returned to the Confederate re-enactor general.

Abrams thought, "It could be make-up, but the officer surely looks authentic."

A shiver ran down Abrams' back.

Abrams spoke," Sir, Do I have the honor of speaking to General James Longstreet, commanding the First Corps of the Army of Northern Virginia."

Longstreet bowed and said," Your obedient servant, sir."

Abrams felt baffled. He had a million questions and no answers.

"It seems we have a bit of a problem, sir. These are the most unusual events. Do you know what caused you and me to be here?"

As if by signal, all sides nodded and started to talk to each other and the opposite side.

"I need time to get some facts. I suggest we meet back here in two hours."

"But before I go, I need to know the positions of your men," Abrams said.

Longstreet flushed and seemed to balk at this request.

"We mean you no harm, sir, "Abrams said. "And given what you have seen of our equipment, we could very easily overcome your unit."

"To further agree with you, general, this whole experience is rather extraordinary to you as me."

Longstreet thought and agreed. He gave Abram's aide a general account of their position in the nearby woods.

When Abrams returned to his copter, his aide told him people were coming to address this situation.

The people would include staff officers from the US Army Special Operations and a Scientist/historian named Wright. He is an expert on this kind of happening. Abrams turned to the aide and wrinkled his brow as if he was amazed. The aide just shrugged and handed Abrams his notebook.

The Group from Washington DC arrived with some data and hand-drawn charts. They tried to explain what had happened.

They concluded that a bend in time had visited Gettysburg, Pennsylvania, last night. It pulled the Confederate troops from 1863 to 2013. While this sounds like science fiction, the scientist/historian explained it had happened before, recently. It was pre-announced by a storm, as the unit experienced. Abrams and his aide read some incident reports concerning this time bend.

Wright told them these incidents occur with the right combination of weather, time, and events during a surge in the earth's electromagnetic field. Wright said he could go on, but it was highly technical and top secret.

Abrams and his aide listened intently; they looked as if they had been shocked by electricity.

The aide asked, "Do you believe this is possible."

That caused the scientist to start over, but Abrams held his hand up and stopped him.

"How am I to explain this to General Longstreet?" Abrams asked no one in particular.

The aide, General Abrams, and the Guard Captain decided on a simple all-purpose explanation that, hopefully, Longstreet would understand. At least, he hoped that Longstreet would get the gist of it.

He would have to persuade Longstreet what he was saying was the truth.

Accompanied by Major Evans of Pentagon Special Operations, He walked out to the middle of the field. He had canvas chairs set under a canopy.

Longstreet arrived with his most trusted aide Major T.J. Goree.

"Go Ahead, Major Evans." Said Abrams.

Major Evans did not talk down to the Confederates. He explained it simply. When he was finished, both Confederate officers expressed disbelief. At one point, Longstreet walked out from under the canopy, took off his hat, shook his head, and gasped.

"Are you gentlemen sure? This sounds like the devil's work," said Goree.

"I assure you this is not superstition, but fact, the truth. The truth is as much as we can know. Frankly, I read and understand it. But sometimes, it seems mumbo-jumbo." Said Evans.

The officers all laughed at the words "mumbo-jumbo."

Evans continued", we are sure this has happened before. Was there anything that seemed odd before you came to this place?"

Major Goree slapped his knee, "yes, last night, the wind. It was a storm such as I'd never encountered. And as I think of it. It was odd that I saw no one as we approached our campsite. I realize now there should have been soldiers on that road. I was too tired to take notice."

The Confederate officers had many questions. Longstreet's main question was: If this extraordinary circumstance happened before? Would it reverse itself?

"Yes, general, we are sure this phenomenon has happened before. The duration of this situation may not be very long." Said Evans.

Major Goree asked," Will it return to the way it was before the storm?"

The question was left hanging in the air. None of the special operation officers knew with certainty. It caused an uncomfortable silence.

The group talked for over an hour. The accents were a drawback. It was hard for Abrams to understand the Confederates with their drawl. At times, all were dismayed. This seemed unreal. They shook their heads in disbelief. They walked out, unable to hear more. Finally, the Confederates sat in resignation.

More coffee was ordered. Each group was asked to use its own utensils and food. It was explained that in modern times, diseases could affect the Confederates. The Guard medical officer checked all food.

However, Captain Browning thought the Confederate food looked better than the guard fare and said so.

Meanwhile, all eyes from both the soldiers in gray and the Guardsmen were on that canopy.

After some particular questions, Major Goree left and returned with a hand-drawn map of the Confederate positions. A guard officer used his phone to take several pictures. The Major rolled up his map and walked away, shaking as if he had just seen a miracle.

Abrams warned the Guard officer, "Captain, you better watch what you do; it may give our guest a heart attack."

After the conference, Abrams explained to General Longstreet that a perimeter had been set all around their position. He explained it was for their good. Any touching of modern equipment or fraternization among soldiers could pass on diseases. A disease that could quickly kill the Confederates.

To which General Longstreet said, "Your world sounds more dangerous than our times."

The area inhabited by the Confederates was sealed off. All Guardsmen were ordered to stay away from the Confederates.

He held a briefing for officers and sergeants; he introduced the team from Washington, DC. They explained the dangers of touching or exchanging goods with the Confederate soldiers.

The scientist said," They have no immunity to our diseases, and touch might eventually kill one or all. While this is an exciting time in our history, they must observe but stay away from it. Even a touch could pass disease. And at the same time, they have illnesses that could be passed on to us, especially if your shots have run out.

Abrams spoke again, "This is a very unusual and historic event. Keep your head on and use good sense. You will turn in all cell phones. It is a matter of national security. Do you understand?"

The men answered in unison, "Yes" The formation broke up in silence. The Guardsmen appeared to understand the significance. They were very interested in the Confederate troops but obeyed the standing orders.

As Abrams returned to his tent, he tried to guess how many Longstreet would take this turn of events, especially since the date was July 2. This was the scene of the Battle of Gettysburg 150 years ago. The significance was overwhelming because Abrams could change history depending on what he said.

As Abrams walked among his men, he reminded the Guardsmen these Confederate soldiers were veterans. Treat them with respect.

Throughout the afternoon, the two sides watched each other through the trees.

Through messengers, it was decided the two sides should talk again. Captain Browning walked to a Confederate picket. He brought a written note because of the thick Southern accents, which were hard to understand.

He handed it to the picket.

The picket saluted and said, "You might as well tell me what you want. I can't read."

The major apologized and read it to the picket. The picket left to deliver the message.

Longstreet and Goree came to the picket line. The Confederate officers insisted on wanting no magic boxes. Goree looked especially at Major Evans, who quickly put his phone in his pocket.

General Abrams had returned with the scientist. The scientist, looking very uncomfortable, cleared his throat and started to speak.

"For unknown reasons, your units, as you know, have been transported to 2013. I am damned if I know what to do about it. Security precautions for your health have been put in place. Everything we will treat and screen before we pass it to you. This will prevent you from catching our time's diseases.

The scientist wanted to say more and ask questions. Abrams felt the questions would embarrass the Confederate officer. Abrams dismissed the scientist.

When the two generals were alone, Abrams handed Longstreet a plastic bag containing a bottle of whiskey.

"This whiskey is said to be your favorite. Abrams said.

Longstreet was clearly touched. He smiled and said, "Kentucky sipping whiskey. I do appreciate this. How did you know?"

Abrams smiled, nodded toward Captain Browning, and said, "We have our ways. Browning is West Point." Browning had done a paper about Longstreet at The Point.

Longstreet turned, saluted Browning, and began to leave the field.

Longstreet turned, looked at Browning again, and said, "Thank you, Captain. I shall put this medicine to good use.

Abrams walked by Browning and whispered, "Well done; I think we did a good thing. Some things never change."

Abrams was met by the scientist, who demanded to ask questions. Against his better judgment, he asked Longstreet and Goree to return to the canopy.

The scientist immediately asked for hair samples.

Goree said, "You are a vulgar little man."

"But I need them for my study. This is a great opportunity." I can write an excellent paper on this event.", answered the scientist.

"We are not some scientific study," said Goree as he left the tent.

Abrams dismissed the scientist.

"I am sorry. He is from a fine university and is quite curious," said Abrams.

Longstreet smiled and said," No need to apologize. He is indulging in his learning. However, I must say he is an ill-mannered man."

Abrams and Longstreet stepped out from under the canopy. They were the same height as their eyes met; their looks showed an understanding. They were becoming friends.

Longstreet sighed and asked," You all know what will happen tomorrow. Is it to be to our advantage? That is if we are back in our time."

Abrams countered," I am not going to answer that until we know more about the effect of this situation and on history."

However, both knew there had to be a reason for the storm. The answer is unknown.

Longstreet nodded knowingly. They saluted and left.

Abrams called a conference in his tent. He wanted to know if the people from Washington knew this divulging information would change history. No one could say with certainty. There were no written records of these occurrences. All the documents were studied and destroyed. They were only oral reports.

As the meeting ended, the scientist asked if he could go to the Confederate camp. Abrams denied the request.

Abrams ordered security increased and helicopters to stay out of the area.

Abrams sat in a Humvee with his staff and listened to the lively discussion and sometimes loud arguments coming from the Confederate camp.

About two hours before sunset, a Confederate officer approached the perimeter. He asked to be passed through. Abrams signaled to a Guardsman to let him pass.

The Confederate officer asked the Humvee driver questions about the working of this carriage. The officer, an engineer, seemed to understand much of the vehicle's operation. Several of the answers were surprising but made sense to the engineering officer.

The young Guardsman asked about the long beards; the Confederate officer chalked it up to style.

"Do they itch?" asked the driver.

The officer answered, "Yes," and laughed. They both laughed.

As Abrams and his staff watched, it was clear soldiering was much the same throughout history. The interest in the other guy's equipment. The questions about beards and uniforms, the ability to share a laugh by each side.

But when the Confederate officer switched to questions about the driver's weapon, the Guardsman pulled back. The officer saw his expression and apologized, and moved toward the perimeter.

The officer turned back, smiled, and said," Much obliged, Billy Yank."

The driver stood, saluted, and answered, Sure thing, Johnny Reb."

The Guardsmen and the Confederates is a watching exchanged smiles. There seems to be a commonality among veterans in them, their soldiering, and their humanness.

The night passed with only one incident. A Confederate soldier got lost and was directed back to his camp by an unseen Guardsman.

The Confederate soldier turned around, trying to find the voice in the night.

As the confederate headed back in the right direction, he said, you must have cat eyes, Yank."

The Guardsman smiled as he re-adjusted the night vision goggles.

The following day, a Guardsman from the perimeter reported two Confederate generals requesting to see General Abrams.

Longstreet was accompanied by another general named Armistead. After introductions, coffee was served, and the Confederate generals had an opportunity to see the Humvee.

Longstreet returned the whiskey bottle empty.

Abrams said, "Gosh, General Longstreet did you drain the bottle?"

Armistead laughed and said, "He would have liked to, but we made his share."

"As a return for your favor, I have given your aide a fine Virginia wine," said Longstreet.

At that point, Armistead said, "Well, go ahead, James, tell him."

Longstreet begins," You are going to shake your head. But given these circumstances, I'd like you to hear me out. One of my officers is a seer. He is fully Cherokee. He has been correct with his predictions many times. He says things will rearrange themselves, shortly and suddenly."

Abrams replied," You know our people say that the atmosphere, I mean weather, is changing too. This could result in the same thing your seer is talking about."

Abrams asked if one of his people could visit the Confederate camp.

"Whom would you sell end, Asked Longstreet.

"Me," said Abrams was to be the volunteer, "but the scientist is itching to go."

"Good Lord, someone might shoot him," said Armistead.

Longstreet said, "In exchange, we would like to send a man to your camp."

It was agreed. Longstreet returned with a Confederate officer in tow. They approached the exchange point and stopped in their tracks. No one moved; they gaped at General Abrams, and the young officer was heard praying.

General Abrams had returned in a hazmat suit.

"Oh, Lord," some said, and all the Confederates stepped back.

Captain Brett Mosser, who had made the first contact with the Guardsmen, was the volunteer.

He balked at the sight of General Abrams.

"Oh my God, general, I can't wear that infernal thing. It will kill me. I swear to you I will die. "complained Captain Mosser.

At that moment, the man in the hazmat suit spoke up.

"Good Lord, it is you, general." Said Longstreet.

"Sure, "replied Abrams. "I've worn these suits many times. I understand the Captain's fears, but if he did not wear it, he could catch one of our diseases and carry them back to your camp."

"It is for your safety and ours, Brett," said Longstreet. "It would be a great shame to miss such an opportunity. I know you to be a brave man, Brett."

The Confederate officer relented and, with much difficulty, was helped into a suit. He had trouble breathing at first, but he handled it in a bit of a while.

With the aid of two Guardsmen, Captain Mosser stumbled, tripped, and then walked into the National Guard position.

"How was he picked?', asked Abrams.

"Short straw," laughed Longstreet.

Abrams walked awkwardly toward the Confederate camp.

Longstreet walked behind, smirking. "Wait till they get a gander at you."

All the activity in the camp stopped as Abrams entered the woods. His image brought even the horses to a standstill. Some soldiers moved away, and some drew close. At first, Abrams was surrounded by soldiers. They stared at the fabric, touching the faceplate and still deciding what to do next.

Abrams said," Excuse me.".

Everyone jumped and moved away. As Longstreet came to Abram's aid, the soldiers moved away quickly.

The best comment came from a Confederate sergeant. He said, "It looks like that man got packaged up."

Longstreet stood back and let Abrams absorb the view.

A banjo started playing. Men milled around by the tent covers. Horses were groomed.

The scene was as if out of a movie: the banjo, the smell of the wood fires, the smell of leather from the saddles, and all the sounds of a camp working. Abrams took it all in. This was, to some extent, similar to other re-enactor events. But this camp had a sense of purpose and urgency. These men were preparing for battle. He felt a grip of sadness, realizing the history about to envelop them.

Longstreet escorted Abrams over to the mess tent. He introduced him to Generals Picket, Pender, and Armistead. Armistead stood and greeted Abrams. Picket, looking like a fancy freelancer, and the overweight and very political Pender eyed Abrams suspiciously.

Abrams said, "Please, Gentlemen continue your mess. I am here for a brief time."

General Pender addressed Abrams with a snarl in his voice," Just what is the purpose of your visit?"

"I guess I wanted to see a different kind of soldiering than I am familiar with.," said Abrams.

Pickett addressed him," I assure you are soldiering is all the same."

"Not from my time. The flare and gallantry have been replaced by brutal destruction.", replied Abrams.

The generals stopped eating, looked up at Abrams, and seemed sure he was speaking the truth. That erased the dismissive attitude of the Confederate generals.

Pickett arose, peered into Abram's faceplate, and asked, "When is this thing going to be over? I need to get back to my division."

Pender, ever-suspicious, said, "How do we know this isn't a Yankee trick."

Armistead intervened, "John, you have seen their weapons and flying things. You better hope the Yankees we are against do not have such gimmicks."

Abrams said," I wish you all a safe journey."

Longstreet detected a note of sadness in Abrams' voice. It silenced all the men in and around the mess tent.

Abrams knew that in less than 48 hours, two of the generals in the tent would be dead.

Longstreet touched Abrams's arm and quietly said," It is time to go. I will see you back."

The two generals walked in silence. Longstreet is hoping Abrams will reveal what he knew.

They met the Confederate Captain, out of his suit and full of news.

He saluted the generals and said," I have seen wondrous things."

He saluted Abrams again and said, "Thank you, general, thank you."

The two generals halted at the perimeter.

Longstreet started, "Will this occurrence end soon?"

Abrams said, "I am told it would happen very soon. I can feel the air changing. There is a mood of strangeness filling the camp.

The generals notice men looking up and acting as if ominous weather was coming.

Longstreet asked if there would be a memory of this experience. Abrams tells him the experts say those from the past will not remember. But we, in the future, may have memories.

Abrams told Longstreet that it had been a distinct pleasure meeting him regardless of the outcome.

Longstreet smiled, nodded, looked at the darkening sky, and said, "We may or may not have something to tell our children about."

Longstreet touched Abrams' arm and said. I will press you again, sir, about our endeavor. Will it be successful? Given the evidence I see, I think it will fail."

Abrams sadly looked at Longstreet and said, "Would it make any difference if you knew the answer?"

Longstreet smiled and said, "No, the die is cast. We will fight despite the consequences."

The generals saluted and ran toward their units.

At that moment, the wind picked up, and the clouds swirled. The sky turned opaque. The storm struck with such force. Trees were uprooted, and soldiers ran for cover; it took the men's breath away.

The lightning flashed so brightly that it looked like a bombardment.

As suddenly as the great cyclone arrived, it was gone. With it, the Confederate camp, It simply disappeared into the storm. And the ground showed no signs of an encampment.

The National Guardsmen were silent. There was a distinct feeling they had lost something. It was several minutes before the Guardsmen started to go about their duties.

The events of those two days marked them. It was confident many Guardsmen would not be the same.

The maneuvers were stopped, and the Guardsmen were transported to a particular area for de-briefing. They were sworn to secrecy under penalty of imprisonment.

All mention of the incident was silenced. All the guardsmen were sent home with a cover story about why the maneuvers were canceled.

Transcripts and recordings were sealed, boxed, and taken to a government's "Where-house" —a place known only to a few in the intelligence community.

General Abrams retired immediately after the case was closed. Interestingly, he visited the grave of General John Longstreet CSA before he went home. He placed flowers on the tombstone and stood quietly talking to the gravestone.

History recorded that the Battle of Gettysburg was fought on July 2nd and 3rd, 1863.

The Confederate army was thrown back, beaten, and never recovered to its previous glory.

As the battle was shaping up on July 3, General Longstreet could not shake a gnawing discontent deep inside. He could not put his finger on it.

It seemed just out of reach and just out of time.

Jonesborough

Marty woke up in a sweat. He had one of those dreams again.

They started after he learned John had died.

John was his best friend. They had met in the army and gone through the war and college together. The funeral was yesterday.

He was awake now, so he thought, "Might as well get up, shower, and head to a business meeting."

He got up, got ready, and headed down the interstate toward Knoxville. After traveling 35 miles, he noticed a sign for historic Jonesborough. John had talked about the town and ought to go sometime. Now was a good time. He decided to stop for breakfast.

Approaching the town, Marty was surprised at the amount of traffic. He had to park at the edge of town. At the Welcome Center, he found out there was a national storytelling festival that morning. That was interesting, but he needed coffee, and the local shops were filled.

He decided to walk to the storytelling area. It consisted of three large white tents on top of a hill. He saw they were selling coffee at one large tent, so he walked in, bought a cup, and sat down.

Suddenly, a woman stepped to the center of the stage to introduce a storyteller. Marty rose to go but bumped into a man sitting beside him; then the storyteller started to talk, so Marty decided to stay put. The storyteller, dressed in a Notre Dame ball cap and guitar, hollered, "Welcome Home, Yankees! Welcome home!" The man next to Marty turned to him, smiled with a soft drawl said, "Welcome home, Yankee."

Marty, in turn, introduced himself.

The man replied, "Tom Jackson, at your service."

Tom Jackson was tall and thin with longish Brown hair. He had bright brown eyes and a sad smile. He had a kindly way about him. Marty seemed drawn to Tom. Tom enjoyed the storytelling.

After the storyteller finished, Marty got up and asked Tom if there was any place to get something to eat.

Tom smiled and answered," Come with me, Yankee."

Tom introduced Marty to fried green tomatoes; they were so good Marty had a second order! "Those were great! Marty said to Tom.

Tom smiled and said, "You see, Yankee, you Northerners merely fill your stomach., We, Southerns, eat!" They sat under a tree, became better acquainted, and fell into easy conversation. They both had left school to join the army; both served in combat.

"I just buried a friend, just like us," said Marty.

"I know what that is like," answered Tom.

"Where do you call home, Yankee?" asked Tom.

"I'm headed to a business meeting, then home to Pennsylvania.

Gettysburg, Pennsylvania." said Marty.

"I know that place," said Tom with a distant look on his face.

Marty asked," How about you?"

"Oh, I live up the hill across from that welcome center," answered Tom

They talked uninterrupted for 20 minutes. It was an easy, relaxed exchange. They discussed life, the army, and storytelling. After that, there was a lull in the conversation.

"Can I ask you a personal question?" asked Marty.

Tom nodded.

"Do you still get the dreams from the war?" Marty continued.

"You mean the dreams that make you think of the smell of sweat, gunpowder, and fear," Tom answered.

Marty just nodded.

"Nah, I don't get those anymore. You have a problem with them, I take it?" asked Tom.

"They have been worse and often since my friend died," answered Marty with a faraway look in his eye.

"You know, Yank? I think I have an idea of how you can settle those dreams. You come with me." Tom said as he stood up and headed toward town.

Tom had a serious expression and said, "In that building is an Indian woman. She makes a bangle that is said to have magic power for dreams. Now, I don't hold with that kind of thing. But many do." said Tom. "You go in there, and I'll just sit here and wait on this bench. I got a lot of very interesting people to look at," smiled Tom.

Marty entered the building, and sure enough, in the very back was a Native American Store. Hesitantly, he walked up to the clerk.

"May I help you? My name is Jane Blair," she said.

"My friend out there said you have something for dreams," Marty whispered.

"Yes, we do. There on the back wall are my dream catchers," she replied.

Marty wore an expression of doubt, and the lady saw that as she pointed the catchers out.

"You see, the dreams are caught in the webbing and destroyed by the sunrise. When parents have tried many ways to help their children's bad dreams, they finally come to me. The dream catcher does its work." explained the lady.

She stopped to turn and look in the direction that Marty was looking.

"You are a veteran!" she said.

"How did you know that?' asked Marty.

"Because the catcher you are looking at is one for a veteran," she continued.

The dream catcher was in two black circles with a blood-red feather in the middle.

She took it, pressed it into his hand, and said," Take it, veteran, it will help. No charge, and bless you".

Rather unsteadily, Marty returned toward the street.

He felt that this circle might work. He found Tom and told him the story.

"Well, I'll be darned. I heard those magic Indian bangles work!" Tom said with a wink.

"I sincerely hope it works for you, "Tom added.

They sat on the bench and talked and laughed together. They spoke of everyday things and family, especially in-laws.

They drew several rather strange looks from the passers-by. We did not mind.

Finally, Tom stood and said he had to get back. "You know Marty. I forgot to ask you what unit you were with.

I was in the First Cavalry," said Marty.

"I was with the 19th Tennessee Infantry. You take good care now, Yankee.

It has been a pleasure," said Tom.

They nodded in agreement. They were going to be friends. Marty reached down to pick up his package. When he turned, Tom was gone, lost in the crowd.

Marty left too. He headed his car toward Knoxville but stopped and called his wife. He talked a little and cried a little.

Instead of going to Knoxville, He turned toward home. That night he asked her if he could hang the dream catcher in the bedroom window.

"Of course!" she answered.

Within two weeks, the dreams were gone, and Marty vowed to return to Jonesborough as soon as possible.

Seven months later, he came back to Jonesborough. He parked and walked up the steep hill across from the Welcome Center.

He stopped at the top and stared.

That is when he realized he had experienced the most extraordinary October day. You don't often hear great storytellers purchase a genuine magic bangle and spend the day with a ghost! At the top of the hill is a grave marker commemorating Tom Jackson, a second-year man from VMI, lst LT, 19th Tennessee Infantry.

Born May 3, 1851, Died July 3, 1863.

Added notes:

The author has a dream catcher, two black circles with a blood-red feather. It was purchased a Jonesborough.

When I tell the story, I end by saying old Tom likes to listen to this story. Here's back there in the shadows. I don't see him, but he's there just the same. He likes you to hear the story too.

MANASSAS

This tale may seem obvious, but don't be too sure.

It was a tour set up by a Northern Virginia Community College history professor. He had taken his Monday, 3-period class to the Manassas Battlefield, commonly called Bull Run.

After a lecture by park rangers, the class was herded out for the walking tour. The ranger was interesting but rigid. He gave emphatic orders to everyone to stay with the group. After talking about a site, the group moved to the next monument. Two of the group held back, and when the others passed out of sight, they bolted to a boundary fence. The woods swallowed them as soon as they climbed over it. They may have made a mistake. The area was overgrown with high bushes and heavy vines. The woods would part, and there were open spaces, larger than clearing. It was hard to believe that so many fought in these conditions, where the trees are close, and visibility is limited.

These two, Mike and Tom, came on the tour for very different and lucrative reasons. Once out of sight, Tom pulled a bag out of his shirt. Armed with rumors, this part of the battlefield had never been thoroughly searched properly in over twenty years. They were there to look for Civil War relics. These items could be sold on the internet for big bucks.

Tom and Mark also enjoyed the hunt, but it was not lost on the men who had died in these woods.

The two began to comb through shrubs, thick bushes, and vines. It made for slow going.

Mark wiped the sweat from his face and questioned Tom about his info.

Tom said, "I am sure; keep going."

Tom began to feel a gloominess brought on by the dark woods.

That is when Tom found a belt buckle. He held it and said, "See."

It was rusted, but you could make out the initials CSA. They both agreed this was a real find.

Now they were motivated. Within minutes, the boys had found a coin, a broken knife, and an emblem from a Confederate hat.

Tom yelped and held up a pistol grip marked with the initials RPT.

I wonder who he was, a reb or a yank, thought Tom.

The students were surprised when they realized they were getting deep into the woods.

Mike checked his watch and said, "We need to return."

"Just a few more minutes," said Tom.

Finally, the two started back toward the visitor's center.

"Wait until the prof sees these," said Tom.

"You know we have to turn them over to the rangers, but what a rush," answered Mike.

"Hold it, do we have to show these to anyone? These are money," said Tom

They were headed back and debating whether to show the loot to anyone.

Mike ended the argument by saying, "Which way?"

The woods turned into a mass of vines, clumps of trees, and brush that hugged their feet. Soon, Tom admitted, he was not sure. He has lost track of the way. They were 50% sure they might be lost. It was now up to 80%.

Tom asked Mike to check his phone for coordinates.

He said, "No signal, you?"

Tom said, "Me neither."

They sat down on a stump to figure this out.

Mike said, "You read the map. You have an idea where we are."

"Nope. And the map is on the bus." Said Tom.

"Tom, let's move up the hill and through those trees. I remember a gulley a little way back." Said Mark.

They found a gulley, but there were better ones.

It was heavy going. The boys stopped to rest. Then they got up and pushed on. It was close to the time to be back at the visitor's center.

"We are lost now, so you take the lead," said Tom.

Mike started in a different direction. They moved as swiftly as they could. They were now officially lost.

"That is it, we need to yell, and someone will hear us," said Mark.

They cupped their mouths and yelled, "Help, help, help!"

As Mike started to yell again, he was cut off in mid-sentence.

Someone standing behind him had his hand clamped over Mark's mouth and a lot of his face. It was a large rough hand.

Tom stood rooted in place. His mouth was open, and his eyes were wide open. Because his mouth was dry, he could not say a word. He was frozen. Whatever was holding Mike scared Tom.

Mike tried to talk to Tom, but it was just enough to breathe.

"Hush up, boy." A voice whispered.

You young in's making enough noise to raise the Devil, his-self", the voice continued.

"If me, I let you go. You promise not to yell again," the voice asked in a low whisper.

Mike nodded The man released Mark.

Mark whirled around to face the voice. It was a giant of a man dressed in gray with a blanket wrapped diagonally around his body. He was wearing a brown slouch hat and held the long rifle the boys had ever seen.

As the man eyed the boys, he said, "Now that ems better. Where did you boys spring from?" Mark answered, "We were looking for relics and got lost."

"Heck, I knew that, and about half the woods knew it too." Said the man as he smiled.

"But you ems ought to be quiet. Thars danger here."

But then, his smile darkened. "You all don't sound like you're from around here."

"Well, no, sir, we are from Pennsylvania," said Mark.

"You all are Yankee kids?" said the man, surprised.

Mark giggled, "Yeah, I guess we are. By the way, that is a cool uniform you got there."

"You daft boy? There ain't nothing cool about this here, wool," The man said. He was becoming angrier.

The two looked at each other, then back to the man, trying to figure out this situation. They turned as if to run.

The man picked up his musket and told the boys to move. They started to run, but he thrust his rifle in their way.

"I said this way." He said.

"OK, but my teacher and the ranger will be looking for us," Mark said.

"You might. You ain't alone." The man said.

He urgently moved them deeper into the wood, prodding them with his musket. "you boys stay in front of me."

The boys were scared and tried to drag their feet, looking for a way out.

A voice came from nowhere, "What do you have there, Caleb?"

The man answered, "I found these Yankee boys about, sir."

A man dressed in a gray but cleaner uniform with shiny buttons and a sash around his waist stepped out of the vines.

The officer looked the two over and said, "You are lost for certain."

"Yeah," mumbled Tom.

Caleb looked at Tom and said, That's sir, boy. This here is Robert Preston Talmage. Ain't you Yankees got any manners."

"Sorry, sir," said Tom. Then he thought about the initials on the pistol grip.

Mark stepped behind Tom and said, "You look great in your uniforms."

Caleb laughed and said, that one told me my uniform was cool. Doesn't that beat it all? "I will take these two in hand. Caleb, move up that hill and keep a sharp eye!" said the officer.

Caleb picked up his musket, saluted the officer, nodded to the boys, and disappeared into the tree line within seconds.

The officer watched Caleb go and turn, "I think I can help you, boys."

He looked the boys over closely. He looked at Tom and Mike's clothes. It seemed as if he had never seen people dressed this way before.

"You head up this hill and try to be as quiet as you can."

The officer heard something, and he tensed.

Abruptly, the officer pulled out his pistol. He whispered, "Don't make a noise."

They could hear movement nearby.

His mood turned anxious, and he nodded toward the tree line and whispered, "Scouts."

He motioned them to start to move. He placed his hand and gun in between the boys.

The large weapon was old-fashioned, colored silver. It had a monogrammed grip, RPT.

Tom checked it out and nodded to Mike. A shiver went down their backs.

The Lieutenant pulled Tom's shoulder and signaled them to stop.

He moved between the boys and pulled them close to him.

"You listen real good. The path you want is at the top of this hill. Be quick and as quiet as possible.

Good luck, Yankees" He smiled and pushed the two forward.

They took four steps and looked back. The officer had fallen. They hesitated and headed back toward the officer.

He was holding his arm. Blood gushed from a wound at the elbow. He waved the boys to run. They passed Caleb on his face as they turned him over. He was dead. His face was half gone, his skin was pinched, and his eyes had an empty look.

"How could this be? We were just talking to him," said Mark.

They panicked and ran. Mike was the first to trip over another body. It took a minute to register that this man was also dead. He lay on his back, clothes ruffled and a sad look on his face. He looked like he was sleeping but for the blood on his uniform.

Tom fell too and found himself lying next to another dead soldier, his face caught in the throes of a painful death. Tom screamed and ran.

There were men trying to help the wounded. A wagon was burning. There was a smell. Sickly sweet smell.

"Oh, my God. We are on the real battlefield." Said Tom.

But it was more like a graveyard.

They continued up the hill dodging torn bodies and broken equipment. The field and hill looked as if the battle had just finished. The carnage was sickening, causing Tom to throw up.

They sprinted toward the top of the hill. Tom had to stop and vomit again.

At the top of the hill, they fell over a bush right into the blacktop path that led to the visitor's center.

Tom and Mark turned to look back, and everybody and everything was gone.

They stepped on top of the stone wall to get a better look. It was all green, trees and brush, no battlefield.

"It is gone," whispered Tom. It couldn't be, but it was. The two just stood and looked.

It Jolted them back into their time. They were scared stiff, literally. They stood on the stone wall, frozen.

They snapped out of their thoughts and ran toward the visitor's center. All they could think to do was to get away. They ran and continually looked back to see if the horror was following. Coming around a turn, they smacked into a park ranger.

"Whoa, where are you headed?" the ranger said.

He quickly realized these were the missing students. "You are in big trouble; get a move now."

The boys were so happy to see someone alive. They hugged the ranger.

The ranger untangled himself and felt the boys shaking.

"Come on, Let's get you to your group."

The group was waiting by the bus, and all were mad. But not as angry as the professor.

The questions started, but the boys talked so fast that no one could understand them.

"Stop, one of you talk."

Tom talked about their find and that the soldiers seemed real, and then they were dead.

"It was awful." Said Mike.

Both were shaking, and it was apparent something had scared them.

Mike and Tom stopped talking when they realized the others were looking at them strangely.

It was apparent the others did not believe them. Yet the two were noticeably scared. Tom was still shaking.

"That is the biggest cock and bull excuse I have ever heard," said the professor.

Tom showed the relics and handed them to the ranger. He and the professor examined them and declared they were real. The ranger's anger eased a little.

The ranger explained that the area was off-limits and had been for years.

"I cannot remember the last time anyone was there." He said.

Once the story was repeated, the group began reconsidering the two's stories. It was still unbelievable.

The class got on the bus. The ranger had the relics and was calling to get help to go through the area.

"How can you explain your story?" asked the professor.

Suddenly, the two yelled, "We are not lying." To some, they seemed to be telling the truth rather than an excusing story.

That night, the boys did not sleep well. They continued to have nightmares.

Tom and Mike were looking for historical relics. They got much more than they bargained for.

Later in the week, as the Rangers swept the area, they found no bodies. However, they found a pistol almost in mint condition. It was from the Civil War era. It was missing a handgrip.

It makes you wonder if a Confederate officer stepped out of history to save a couple of Yankee boys.

Veterans

February 8, 2008.

In Iraq, an American patrol is ambushed. Their vehicles, a truck, and a Humvee, were put out of action within minutes.

The soldiers and interpreter scrambled to a ditch backed by a rock ridge. From this enforced ditch, the group prepared to defend themselves.

Their situation was precarious. Three men were wounded, the ammo was getting low, and the radio could not raise any friendly forces.

Iraq turned dark.

The eight men pooled their ammo and water and cared for the wounded. The interpreter volunteered to try to get help. He was forced back to the ditch by sniper fire.

The ridge line opened into a vast desert that the Iraq troops surely had covered.

The interpreter alerted the patrol leader that the Iraqis were moving in for an assault. The Iraqis were calling insults and shooting to get the Americans to fire back.

The shooting was to get the patrol to give away their exact positions.

The patrol prepared for the worst. And it came. A vicious but brief firefight sent the Iraqis back.

The patrol leader checked the men. One more was wounded.

"Stay low, keep quiet. That was only round one," he said

All at once, the men heard rustling up on the ridge.

"They are behind us." Said a soldier.

"Impossible!" answered the interpreter. "It has to be animals."

"I hope you are right."

The sound seemed closer.

Two of the patrol turned and aimed their weapons at the ridge line.

A voice was heard saying, "How are you all doing?' We thought we'd come and help."

From the left side of the ridge, another voice said, "Yes, sir, we are here too."

These were American voices.

The patrol wanted to cheer. But the Iraqis were starting to move forward.

Voices spoke almost at once. "Front rank kneel, present" and "Pick your targets, boys."

As the Iraqis broke cover, a volume of fire from the ridge lit the area. The sound and light stunned the Iraqis.

They fell back.

The voices on the ridge said, "Load up, boys. They will be back. "Yes, indeed"

"Who are those people? and what about that firepower." "Wow."

"Keep calm," the patrol leader said.

He turned to the ridge and yelled, "Thank you, and who are you?"

There was no answer.

Quickly the voices on the ridge called to make ready.

"Unit present; fire at my command." The left-side voice said.

"Get ready; they do not know what they are in fur." The right side shouted.

The men on the ridge waited. The Iraq assault was so close the patrol could see their faces.

The command "Fire" was lost in the amount of flame that erupted from the ridge.

The Iraqis' assault stopped, and they ran back to cover. But another group to the left opened fire. The sound of vehicles was heard.

The Iraqis did not stop at their primary position but ran past it into the darkness.

Ten minutes later, a British column drove up to the patrol. After pats on the back and handshakes. The American patrol leader said," How did you find us by radio?"

"No, Sargent, it was that blast of fire. Where did you get such weapons? I, nor my Sargent, have seen such fire from weapons before."

"It was not us. Those guys on the ridge." They saved us." answered the American.

"Well then, let's find out who your saviors are," said the British officer as he and two American soldiers climbed the ridge.

The three return, puzzled. They found no sign of anyone on both sides of the ridge.

"Nothing but the smell of black powder." Said a soldier. "And I know that has not been used since the Civil War."

In the morning, a search was done again. They did find a Union soldier's cap and a Confederate belt buckle from a pack.

They were more puzzled than ever. The British and American soldiers wrote a similar report and sent them to Headquarters with the hat and buckle.

The objects disappeared. The Headquarters made fun of the report, citing it as a tall tale.

But the ordinary soldiers knew and believed it happened. The story was carried back not by news journalists or in action dispatches but by the soldiers themselves. A new addition to the legends with "A Twist".